Arne Mikkelsen

Rita Rabelais

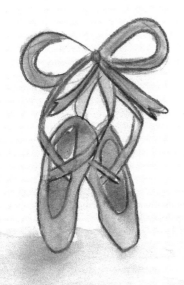

Night, Night, Sleep Tight, Little Ballerina

Written by Rita Rabalais
Illustrated by Anne Michele Erwin

Night, night,
Sleep tight,
Little Ballerina!

The day is done,
You've had such fun,
tiny ballerina.

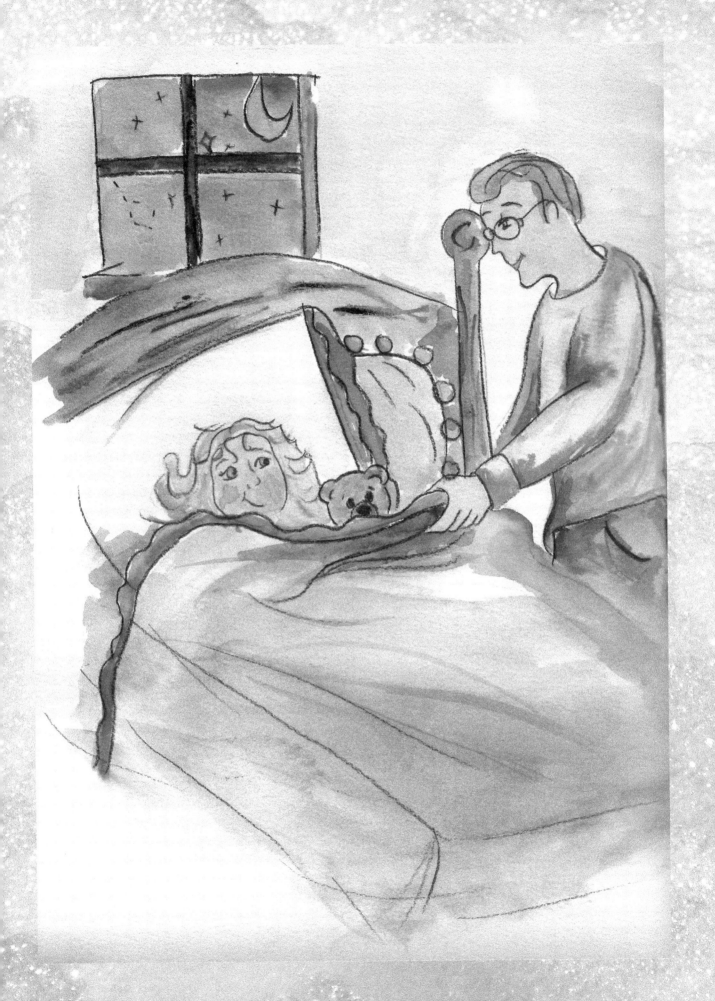

Early this morning
You rolled out of bed.
Sweet dreams and stardust
Still danced in your head.

PJ's off and thrown
In the top drawer
'Cause mama said PJ's
Don't belong on the floor!

A pink sparkly t-shirt
And a homemade tutu
All poofy and puffy
Made especially for you.

You pranced down the stairs
One
Two
Three
And
Four
Turned the corner and
Glided across the floor.

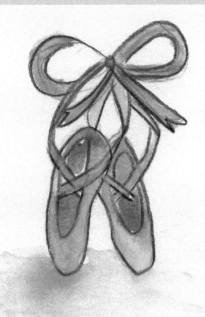

Into the kitchen,
Ten toes leading the way,
Ready to dance through
A bright sunny day.

The kitchen was filled
With warmth and sweet smells
Mama kissed your cheek
As you heard the church bells.

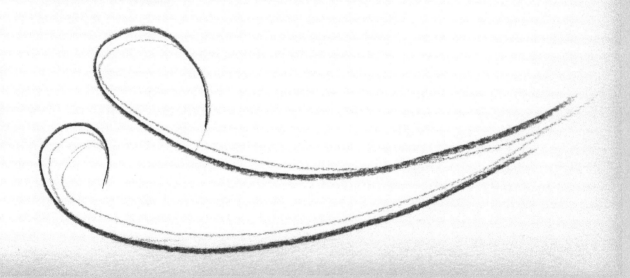

You followed the music
As it floated on air.
Sunshine and promises
Blowing through your soft hair.

The sidewalk beckoned
And you heeded its call
Dancing with autumn breeze
As red and gold leaves fall.

You met your best friends
Waiting down the street
The three of you twirled
On six little feet.

Spinning and giggling
And playing all day
Bent knees over toes
A perfect plie!

Jumping and whirling
Lovely pirouettes
Helping each other
If someone forgets.

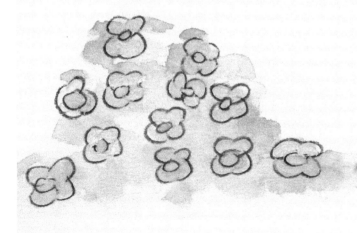

Playing and dancing
Minutes turn to hours.
Time for little ones
To go home for showers.

You're cozy and warm
In you soft PJ's.
One last pirouette,
As the radio plays.

Your eyes are heavy.
The last page is read.
Dad tucks in your quilt.
You're all snug in bed.

Then mommy and daddy
Kiss you on your cheek.
Whispering so softly,
You hardly hear them speak,

Night, night,
Sleep tight,
Little ballerina.

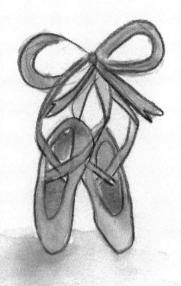

The End

Rita Youngblood Rabalais is a retired elementary school teacher, wife, and mother. Traveling with her husband is her favorite thing to do, but Louisiana is home sweet home. She is the author of *Seventy Times Seven*, *The Piano's Song*, and *Walking on Wings*.

Anne Michele Erwin is a junior at C.E.Byrd High School in Shreveport, Louisiana. This is her first time illustrating a book. She loves expressing herself through art, and plans to use her creative talents in her future career.

CPSIA information can be obtained
at www.ICGtesting.com
Printed in the USA
JSHW021048121120
9456JS00008B/105